Who Loves To Count on The Farm?
1 to 10

by Sandra Sarver

illustrated by B. Lemaire

Copyright © 2014 Sandra Sarver
All rights reserved.

Case IH tractor images by permission. Copyright © 2014
CNH Industrial America LLC. All rights reserved.
Case IH is a trademark registered in the United States and many other countries,
owned by or licensed to CNH Industrial N.V., its subsidiaries or affiliates.

Nebraska logo used by permission. Copyright © 2014
University of Nebraska-Lincoln. All rights reserved.

ISBN: 1499298617
ISBN 13: 9781499298611
Library of Congress Control Number: 2014908220
CreateSpace Independent Publishing Platform
North Charleston, South Carolina

Visit www.wholovesthefarm.com or www.amazon.com to order additional copies.

Who Loves to Count on the Farm? 1 to 10

by Sandra Sarver

illustrated by B. Lemaire

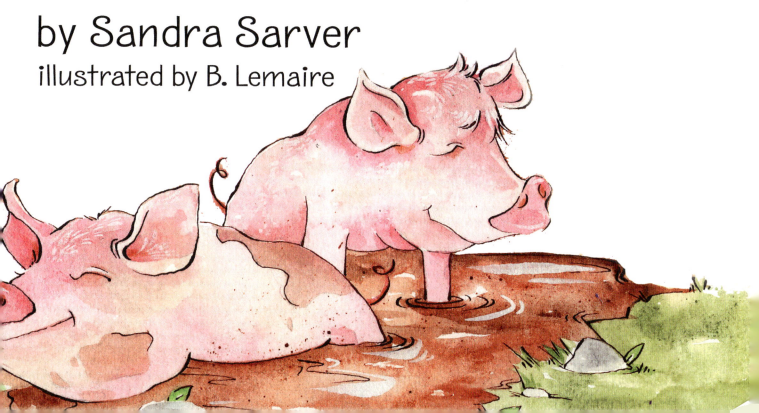

one red tractor

two majestic horses

three muddy pigs

four playful dogs

5

five friendly goats

6

six curious cats

7

seven grazing cows

eight wooly sheep

nine baby chicks

10

ten colorful flowers
ten beautiful butterflies

Do you love to count on the farm?
1 to 10

1 one

2 two

3 three

4   four

5   five

6   six

7 seven

8 eight

9   nine

10   ten

Made in the USA
Charleston, SC
21 November 2016